To Wash One's Hands

BY

MICHAEL JOHN PETTY

TO WASH ONE'S HANDS
By Michael John Petty

Copyright © 2025, 2026 Michael John Petty
Bright Morning Star Press
All rights reserved.

ISBN: 979-8-9951173-0-8

This is a work of fiction. Although this story chronicles the historical events surrounding the crucifixion of Jesus Christ, this is an artistic rendering of the events. Names, characters, places, and incidents are either the product of the author's imagination or are used fictitiously.

To request permissions, contact the publisher.

"Ecce Homo," aka "Behold the Man,"
by Antonio Ciseri, 1871

All scripture quotes, namely in the form of dialogue, are derived from the English Standard Version of the Holy Bible.

Cover design by Michael John Petty

*To my Lord and Savior,
the Bright and Morning Star.*

Soli Deo Gloria

Introduction

The Bible is full of fascinating characters. There are kings and conquerors, shepherds and fishermen, nobles and paupers. For every David there is a Saul. For every Esther, a Jezebel. Yet even the most heroic and moral of these are imperfect—all except One. While the scriptures speak of the ultimate triumph of good over evil, a victory that can only be won by God Himself, there are moments in time when it seems that all hope is lost. It seems as if night will never again be shattered by daybreak.

This is the case when Jesus is betrayed into the hands of the religious elite. These chief priests, scribes, and elders would sooner see the self-appointed Son of Man crucified than recognize their own pride and lust for power. But it was not the fault of the Jews only concerning Christ's death. The Gentiles played their part as well, and none was so directly involved in these events as the historic Roman governor, Pontius Pilate.

The prefect of the region that was once the Kingdom of Israel, Pilate is an interesting figure. History tells us that he was a cruel man. Both the Jewish historian Josephus and the Roman historian Tacitus recount his part in the death of Christ, not to mention other violent actions during his time in office. However, scripture itself seems to paint Pilate as being far more complicated.

I've always thought that Pilate was one of the more tragic characters in the Bible. Not only does he seem to believe Jesus' innocence, but he is even willing to let the Man go. Indeed, Pilate comes so close to doing the right thing before he ultimately (and tragically) caves in to the demands of the Jewish people. I've always wondered what was going on in Pilate's mind during Jesus' trial, as the Jews screamed for his immediate death.

What did he really think about Jesus? Why was he so fearful of the people? Was he haunted by his decision?

Truthfully, we can never know.

Before you dive into this short story, heed this disclaimer first. *To Wash One's Hands* is inspired by the New Testament narrative, pulling from Jesus' interactions with Pilate in all four Gospel accounts—Matthew, Mark, Luke, and John—to create a seamless order of events. However, this is a purely fictional work, utilizing artistic license to dive into the mind of Pontius Pilate. While we will never know this side of eternity what actually occurred in the man's thought-life during these events, this is a supposal of what *may* have been, whether in whole or in part.

As someone who struggles with many artistic renditions of Christ, I'd like to make something else clear to those still on the fence: I have taken careful steps to ensure that Jesus Himself does not stray from the same Son of God we read about in scripture.

All His dialogue comes directly from the English Standard Version (ESV) translation. Though many characters around Jesus have lines that are not found in the text (lines that I hope will only emphasize the scriptures rather than distract from them), Christ only speaks the words you would read in your Bible. This is by design.

Additionally, I highly encourage you, dear reader, to pore over the biblical account for yourself.

Jesus' conversations with Pilate can be found in all four Gospels, specifically in Matthew 27, Mark 15, Luke 23, and John 18. If you have not read them before now, stop reading this and do so. The context matters, and it will inform the rest of the story. Afterwards, feel free to read them again and see how *To Wash One's Hands* compares. Hopefully, you will see the continuity between them.

To Wash One's Hands

There was nothing uncustomary about that morning. The sun rose like any other, glistening over the palms and waking the parched desert land. Light stretched out across the stone and sand, awakening the color that the night had once buried. The coarse air had yet to burn, and in the cool of the dayspring, a soft breeze could be felt. It was as satisfying as a dip in a natural spring, though the relief was short-lived. Perhaps the only thing of note was the noise.

Even at dawn, the city crackled like a brood of cicadas rising from the east. It was the week of Passover, and the Day of Preparation at that. The Sabbath drew near, and many of the Jews from across Judea had traveled to Jerusalem to make their sacrifices and celebrate. Celebrate what? Pontius Pilate did not fully know or understand, nor did he care. The Roman prefect had lorded over this region for several years now, though in that time he had ignored most of the Jewish customs. As was his custom, he had come from his home in Caesarea to ensure that peace was enforced, nothing more. Even during their holy days, he believed that these people must remember their place.

Maybe especially then.

There had been enough unrest since he had taken over from Valerius Gratus. Many of the zealots were still active across the region. Their misguided attempts to overthrow the Roman guard were just that. *They had not a prayer to the gods,* Pilate thought, *let alone the One they claim looks over them.* This single God, they say, had delivered this people centuries ago from the hands of Egypt, Babylon, and Persia. After centuries of overcoming their enemies, it seemed that Rome had done what so many empires failed to. They had beaten the Hebrews, yet there was still much unrest.

There was no other choice but for Pilate to show his face to those gathered in Jerusalem, precisely during these tumultuous times. He desired to instill fear in them, to keep order when disorder ran rampant.

These thoughts plagued his mind as he wandered the courtyard. It was early, and he had awoken with no sleep left in him. The trees and palace walls stood as guards for his thoughts, keeping any unwelcome illuminance at bay. He wondered, then, if Apollo ever slept. *Did the gods need rest?* Augustus Caesar—*may he live forever*—had once been deemed *Divi Filius*, a title his successor had also taken upon himself. His coin was famously inscribed, "Divine Caesar and Son of God." Yet, Pilate had been told that even Caesar slept.

If gods can sleep, and gods can die, how are they any different from the rest of us?

This was a question for another time. The Jews' holy week was almost over, and Pilate took comfort in the truth that he would be free of this city soon enough. At least for a while. If only it were not so divided, he believed that Jerusalem may have been a paradise. A land set apart for pleasure and purpose. Yet now it was only the domain of cheap merchants, endless beggars, diseased prostitutes, and religious idealists who sought more to share in Pilate's power than they did to worship their own God. *Hypocrites, the lot of them.*

It was sure enough that these Jewish elites were on Pilate's mind as a commotion formed at the gate. One of the guards spoke with the offenders causing the disturbance, desperate for the prefect's attention, but Pilate retired indoors. There was no need for his presence. It was his view that the people were here to scold him yet again for the supposed profaning of their temple, a monument to their past victories. If it would not have caused such a stir among them, Pilate would likely have devoted the temple to destruction himself.

It wasn't long before one of his centurions entered the praetorium. The man, known by many as Longinus, looked to Pilate with distress. "My lord, your presence has been requested by the Sanhedrin."

The prefect stole a sip from the fruit of the vine, forcing the Jews to further anticipate his arrival. "Did they state their business, or is this a social visit?"

"They say they have a prisoner whom they wish to see brought to justice."

"Oh?" This was quite curious to Pilate. Rarely did the Jews turn on one of their own. Certainly not to him directly. On occasion, the Sanhedrin brought forth those they could not punish by law themselves, but this sounded different. Intrigue got the better of him. "And who is this man?"

"If he is who I think he is, my lord, he is one of the most famous men in Jerusalem. Perhaps the whole region."

Wasting no more time, the doors were opened to him as Pilate stepped out of the palace. He was tired from his restlessness but rendered no signs of fatigue. There were more of them gathered in the courtyard than he had expected, all of whom looked as if they were ready to stone the man themselves. This man, who stood before the Roman official, wore a blackened mark across his face. He was held in chains by the temple guard as Pilate's own centurions stood nearby. They had dealt unkindly with him already but likely hoped that Rome itself might deal in horrors far worse. If he were guilty, they would be right.

"What accusation do you bring against this man?" Pilate demanded, cutting the pleasantries.

They all began to speak at once. Each man chattered over the other, all emphatic that this prisoner of theirs was some sort of criminal. He did not look like the normal Jewish rubble that Pilate was used to punishing, but it was hard to tell beneath the scrapes and bruises. One thing the prefect did know was that it was far too early for this mindless drivel. Within moments, his guards secured the peace.

"Oh prefect, we beseech thee!" said one of the chief priests, stepping forward. Remembering all their names was impossible. This one wore a thick, gray beard that fell halfway to the ground, though he dressed like all the others. He was articulate, and Pilate recognized him from prior dealings. One of Joseph ben Caiaphas' top men, he believed. "We found this man misleading our nation and forbidding us to give tribute to Caesar."

"He spoke blasphemies!" another interrupted.

The chief priest spoke again. "He said that he himself is

the Christ. A king!"

Pilate looked upon the beaten man. He did not look like a king. In truth, he did not look like much of anything at all. The man stood there quietly, no look of anger in his face, no rage beneath his broken eyes. There was no fear either. No protest. He stood there as still as if they were not speaking of him at all.

"If this man were not doing evil, we would not have delivered him over to you," the priest concluded, appearing somewhat vexed himself at the prisoner's lack of dissent.

"Take him yourselves and judge him by your own law." Wasn't this why Gratus had installed Caiaphas in the first place? So as not to hear these endless debates and trivial blasphemies that were of no consequence to Rome? "I have no need to hear of this further."

Pilate turned back to his chambers, wishing to recuse himself from this plainly fabricated matter. It had occurred to him that this was the Jesus of whom he had heard so much about. The same miracle man that the people loved. The supposed prophet who wandered the streets, who rode in on an ass to enormous fanfare and high praise not days earlier. He was undoubtedly responsible for sending the Pharisees, Sadducees, and their ilk to greater heights of envy and strife. His guard had reported about the unrest among the religious elite, noting their debates with this man across the city. He had even caused them to stumble in interpreting their sacred laws.

Pilate felt some small satisfaction in hearing that.

However, the Jews could deal with their own problems. As prefect, Pilate was here to ensure peace in Jerusalem and to prevent another riot. That was all.

Twice already had the Jews fought against him. The first was after he had moved the imperial standards into the city. Protesters swarmed his home for days. Even under threat of death, they offered up their lives willingly, if only to make a point about Pilate's apparent offense. The message had been received then, and he—perhaps uncharacteristically—showed them mercy for their devotion. Perhaps that had been a mistake. Later, the people revolted after a new aqueduct had been commissioned. It was with the help of many of the Jews that Pilate secured the necessary funds from their temple's treasury for this development. But the religious elite could not control the people, and a mob quickly arose. Many died as a result, and Rome was not pleased.

There had been several other disagreements over the years, mostly concerning their ceremonial laws about idols and sacrifices. It seemed to Pilate that these people were never satisfied with his rule. It was no wonder that they had once appealed directly to Caesar—and he had been careful ever since. Careful to enforce the rule of law while allowing the chief priests and scribes the authority to oversee much of their flock. He knew when to get involved and when to turn his face away.

This was a dispute they could settle on their own. They had the power to do with this Jesus what they ought to. He had no desire to be a part of it.

"It is not lawful for us to put anyone to death," the priest spoke again, a short snarl escaping the man's rapacious lips.

Pilate held his peace. The Hebrew was right. This was not a privilege granted to the Jews, and they knew it. Only Rome could execute those deemed a true threat to the empire. Only Rome had the power to release death on its enemies. Pilate turned back to the Sanhedrin, who were anxious to hear his reply.

"Bring him to me."

The centurions took the prisoner from the Jewish leaders, and they followed close behind as Pilate entered the praetorium. He motioned for his guards to shut the door behind him. He did not want the Sanhedrin to overhear. They would not dare enter his home, a palace adorned by the gods themselves, in fear of rendering themselves unclean according to the trivial standards of their law. It mattered not to Pilate. He wished to speak to this Jesus on his own.

The man stood silent. He spoke not a word, and his breath was quite shallow. The night had not been kind. A cheek stained with blood. Ragged, dirty clothes. Pilate observed that he appeared to have been tossed to and fro like a bound slave falling behind on a caravan.

"Are you the King of the Jews?"

He said nothing at first but then looked to Pilate with a heaviness that he could not fathom. The man, this Jesus, spoke with authority that would have rivaled Pilate's own if he had not been shackled. Had he raised his voice, it may have even been threatening.

"You have said so."

"So, you are a king then?"

"Do you say this on your own accord, or did others say it to you about me?"

"Am I a Jew?" A quick swig cleared the throat and stalled Pilate's budding laughter. "Your own nation and the chief priests have delivered you over to me. What is it that you have done?"

"My kingdom is not of this world," the man said with a calmness that transcended his disheveled appearance. It was quite unsettling to witness. Pilate had never met a man like this before, a man seemingly uninterested in his own freedom. "If my kingdom were of this world, my servants would have been fighting, that I may not be delivered over to the Jews."

This Jesus was a curious one. One moment he seemed to deny being a king, but the next he claimed to rule over some foreign kingdom outside of Rome. Which kingdom? He could not say. Could it be a secret Hebrew sect that the imperium was yet unaware of?

"But my kingdom is not of this world."

"So, you are a king, then?"

"You say that I am a king," Jesus spoke. "For this purpose, I was born, and for this purpose I have come into the world, to bear witness to the truth. Everyone who is of the truth listens to my voice."

This man wasn't a prophet. He was mad. It was clear that the beating he had endured had broken something in his spirit. This Christ spoke in riddles and parables that would send the heart to doubt. It was no wonder that the Pharisees hated him.

Pilate scoffed. "What is truth?"

The man didn't answer. He had no more to say; that

much was clear. The ramblings of a lunatic were hardly enough to put him to death, nor would it be worth the trouble the day before the Sabbath. It was surprising that the Jews themselves wouldn't have waited until after their feasts had concluded. An extended trial would have certainly lasted through their religious observances, though it made no difference to Pilate. For the Roman, death may come at any time, and taking a life on the Jewish Sabbath would be no different than to do so on the first day of the week.

This whole trial was predacious. Perhaps the Jews hoped that Pilate would scare Jesus off, that he would put the fear of the gods into him. Maybe since they couldn't bait him themselves, they had hoped that he could as the governing authority. He once more tried to reason with the man.

"Do you not hear how many things they testify against you?"

Jesus stood there as if a statue, and Pilate was amazed. There was nothing remarkable about him. He was not particularly handsome, though surely his mother would have thought differently. He was rugged, filthy, and had seemingly no friends to call his own. Nobody was present to protest these claims. And yet, he spoke with such a conviction that it could not be denied. It was utterly incomprehensible. Any other "hero of the people" would have plead valiantly for his life.

It was as if he were giving it willingly.

Even so, he was not Pilate's problem. Soon after, they returned to the crowd of anxious priests, scribes, and elders, murmuring amongst themselves like beasts.

"I find no fault in this man."

The Jews erupted, this time in more of an uproar than before. Each member of the Jewish council hurled their own accusations against Jesus. Charges of blasphemy, violence, sedition, and treason fell from their lips like warm milk from the mouth of a babe. As locusts, they piled together for the sake of destruction, all centered on this one man.

Longinus called for order, and within moments it was so.

"Our apologies, prefect," the long-bearded priest

pleaded. "He stirs up the people, teaching throughout all Judea, from Galilee even to this place..."

"Galilee, you say?"

The priest nodded. "Yes."

Pilate turned to Jesus. "You are a Galilean, then?"

He didn't answer, but the priest quickly confirmed his suspicions.

"Herod is here in the city; did you not know this?" They muttered amongst themselves. "Take him to Herod and tell him that I have personally sent you to receive his counsel. If the man is a Galilean, he should be judged by him."

"Of course, prefect." The priest said, the temple guards seizing Jesus once more. "We will consult Herod on this matter. Thank you for your wisdom. May your rule be blessed."

As Pilate returned indoors, the guards saw to it that the Sanhedrin and their prisoner were removed from the grounds. Pilate had dispatched a few guards to ensure they arrived at Herod's court in one piece.

That would certainly be enough.

Making his way down the hall, Pilate's servants met him with pleas to join his wife for breakfast. He considered the request but denied. After this strange encounter, he was no longer hungry and so instead he wandered the halls.

As he ambled down the heated stone, Pilate's mind continued to return to Jesus. This man would not leave his thoughts. This man who claimed to be a king from another realm—another world. It was as if he were claiming to be one of the gods, clothed in the flesh of a man. There were legends, of course, legends that the gods once walked among men. But only Caesar could be called the son of the gods; only he could be said to rule a kingdom beyond this world.

This Jesus came from a foolish people who worshiped only one God. They believed that a single divine being was all that was necessary to oversee every aspect of the cosmos. Pilate could not fathom it. This man was certainly afflicted by some disease that poisoned his mind. He was likely no threat, not even to the Jewish priests and scribes, but they were quite fastidious when it came to their laws and customs. If this man claimed to come from the divine, they would dispose of him in any way they could. Anything less would threaten their hold over the people.

Pontius Pilate tried to put the whole thing out of his mind.

Pilate's usual duties filled the rest of his morning. He was briefed by his men stationed around the city, having been informed about some of the rowdier groups who may have posed a threat. They had recently caught one zealot, a murderer who had caused quite a stir among the people. He was responsible for inciting many to violence against the "occupiers" who had conquered their land. Pilate was thankful he was off the streets.

These people claimed to serve a God who had fought on their behalf, a God that supposedly gave them this land as their own. If this were true, then why had he allowed them to fall to Rome's "inferior" gods? How had this single God of the Hebrews failed to protect his people? Pilate could not help but contemplate these things as he aimlessly attended to his daily routine. He could not wait to get out of the city and back to his home in Caesarea. He wished to see the sea again, to look out across the domain of Neptune and bask in the peaceful glories of this region. Aside from the people, he quite enjoyed the land itself, especially the closer he was to the sea. But there was nothing glorious about this desert, and he had grown to hate these city walls.

Pontius Pilate was not sure how much time had passed when he was interrupted once more by his guard.

"My lord?"

"Yes, what is it?"

"It is the Sanhedrin, my lord. They have returned."

Pilate scowled. "For what purpose? Do they have another prisoner?"

The guard shook his head. "No, sir. Jesus of Nazareth is still with them. Men from Herod also."

Pilate rose and darted across the stony hall. When he arrived at the open doors, a silence fell over the Sanhedrin. Jesus was now garbed in what could only be described as royal clothing, surely an attempt at mockery. In the presence of Herod's men, Pilate did not first address the Jews. Instead, he signaled to the new guards, clad in scaled armor. One of them stepped forward.

"Greetings from Herod Antipas, prefect," he spoke. "We come to deliver this Jesus of Nazareth back to you."

Pilate took a good look at the beaten man in chains and then back to Herod's men. "May I ask why?"

"The tetrarch has considered this man but wishes to defer to your judgment, prefect. He appreciates the unique position you hold."

This surprised Pilate. He and Herod had rarely seen eye to eye when it came to law and order. On a previous occasion, Pilate had stepped on the ruler's toes, having killed several Galileans. This was an error that he had hoped to correct, and thus he had no trouble sending Jesus to Herod in return. Though the tetrarch's personal scandals appalled him, there were strictly political reasons to ensure there was peace between them.

"My lord wishes to convey the deepest respects to you

and your status," the servant continued. "He only hopes that you will see this as a sign of good faith."

"Tell Herod that I accept his offering and that I wish to meet with him soon, after all of this is done. Perhaps then we can discuss a further allegiance."

Herod's men bowed and then left. The Sanhedrin, their guards, and Jesus remained. Pilate turned to the Jews before him and waved his hand.

"We will reconvene at my judgment seat. Then, we will discuss this Jesus of Nazareth."

Pilate did not wait for any response or rebuttal. Instead, he returned to the praetorium, and his men shut the doors behind him. Sweat from the desert heat dripped like dew from his crown, and the soles of his feet ached as he walked down the open hall. The further Sol climbed in the heavens, the hotter the days became. He yearned to bathe in the cool graces of Neptune and dreamt of the rising tide. But there was no sea here, not in this sanded waste.

He climbed to the next level before stopping abruptly at a window that overlooked the city. As he glanced at Jerusalem, a weary sigh escaped his lips. He looked at the walls that surrounded them and then the people, who weaved through the narrow streets like ants. It was his burden to rule, and these were the days that came with that burden. Pilate felt a heaviness upon him. It was the same feeling he had when speaking with the Nazarene in private earlier. He was troubled by the return of this man.

How could so many fail to arrive at a clear judgment concerning him?

What had kept a consensus from being formed?

Who was this man, really?

Pilate had to speak someone about this, though he trusted no one to give him wise counsel. Even if Tiberius himself had been present, he may have evaded his guidance in favor of something more divine. Though, what type of man could be more divine than Caesar?

The prefect wandered further down the hall and found refuge in the lararium. The room was painted with visages of the gods, the embodiments of strength, honor, and wisdom. He had been told the stories of this mythic pantheon since his youth and had clung to them tightly when in modes of distress. Yet, when Pilate's eyes met Mars, a hollow silence was his reply. War was not what he was seeking; it was peace that he needed. Peace would get him through his time in Jerusalem, and only peace would get the Jewish leaders off his back.

Pilate knelt before the Lar enshrined above him. It was a small idol, made of bronze, that held up one hand in comfort while the other rested firmly at its side. The prefect muttered a request for wisdom. Over and over, he repeated the very same idle words, wondering if the gods would grant him favor or abandon him altogether. It all soon became mindless, and Pilate was quickly swept up in his thoughts. The heaviness had not left him, and the gods had not offered any sign of aid. He took a deep sigh and rose to his feet.

It was best to simply get this over with.

The Sanhedrin had complied with Pilate's orders and followed his guards to the stone pavement, a place they called Gabbatha. By the time the prefect had arrived, a crowd had formed, surely made up of the chief priest's most devoted followers. It hadn't occurred to Pilate that many across the city may be following this trial beyond his gates. Perhaps some had even followed Jesus through the night. Considering the man's infamy across not just the city but all of Judea, this should have been expected. The ceaseless chatter he had thought simply concerned the people's Sabbath preparation seemed to have been, in truth, centered on the Galilean. A Nazarene.

Pilate sat on his throne and ordered that a bowl of cold water be brought to him. It felt as if he were Caesar himself, looking out over the masses. He would never have admitted this publicly, of course. He was only a small component in the larger body that was Rome. A man fully and completely replaceable, as his predecessor had been. Still, he relished the importance his status brought him, even if the burden was often heavier than he was comfortable with.

Within moments, the man Jesus was brought before Pilate, though he avoided looking the beaten man in the eye. It was an unsettling picture, and the growing masses had captured most of his attention. An audience like this would bring scrutiny on whatever decision Pilate made, and the people seemed restless. It didn't help that many of the religious leaders had made their way into the crowd.

The prefect turned to see the long-bearded priest from before, now standing at the foot of the raised platform that separated Pilate from the commoners. Pilate grinned knowing that this man had no choice but to look up at him. Then, he addressed the Jewish council gathered there.

"You brought me this man as one who was misleading the people," Pilate began. As he spoke, a silence befell the crowd. Everyone intently listened to his words. "And after examining him before you, behold, I did not find this man guilty of any of your charges against him. Neither did Herod, for he sent him back to us."

A grumbling rolled out from among the people, and Pilate could sense the displeasure among the Sanhedrin. They hated this man far more deeply than he had imagined. There was nothing particularly threatening about this Jesus. By all accounts, he was not a zealot; he was a peaceful man. Yes, there had been rumors that once, maybe twice, the Nazarene had brought a whip into the temple and frightened off the merchants there, but Pilate could see no reason why this would strike such deep discord between them. *Was this Jesus not also a Jew? Did he not also follow their laws?*

"Nothing deserving death has been done by him," the prefect continued. "I will therefore punish and release him." This seemed to be a fair compromise. An example would be made of this Jesus. The religious elites would surely be satisfied with that. Likewise, he would not be killed, which would keep the rest of the people, and especially his zealous followers, from any outrage.

What happened next surprised Pilate. He was not shaken when the chief priests, scribes, and elders began to curse him for his ruling. Nor was he particularly shocked when some of their allies in the crowd did the same. But it soon became clear that the people themselves were dissatisfied with his verdict, and any hopes for simple peace were dashed instantaneously. Murmuring turned to shouting, and the crowds began to thunder.

"You have a custom that I should release one man for you at the Passover," he spoke again, hoping to calm them. "Would you have me release unto you the King of the Jews?"

As he spoke, Pilate could see the priests and elders slither among the crowd, whispering in the people's ears. Like serpents, they preyed upon them as the masses started to hail out curses of their own. Some even began to accuse the ruler of treason. None of them wanted to see Jesus of Nazareth released. Instead, many of them called for someone far worse.

"Away with this man!" one of them shouted.

"Release to us Barabbas!" cried another.

There was no way that the people would have wished Barabbas free rather than Jesus. *Did this man not receive enormous fanfare just days ago?* Still, here the people of Jerusalem were, chanting the name "Barabbas" as if it were one of their daily prayers. The man, if one could truly call him a man and not simply a beast, was a robber. No, he was more than that. He was an insurrectionist and a murderer responsible for many deaths across the city. Barabbas—who in full was named Jesus Barabbas, though he was always referred to exclusively by his surname—was a horrid man, one whom Pilate had sentenced to death for his crimes.

Indeed, Barabbas had been one whom the Jewish elite had no trouble disavowing in public, and none of them protested his pending execution before now.

Anger flooded the prefect's mind, and soon Pilate's vision was blurred. The people had become insufferable. To prefer a hardened criminal to a wandering preacher? It was maddening. He rose and scolded them.

"Whom do you want me to release for you: Barabbas or Jesus, who is called Christ?"

The response was overwhelming, and Pilate could not believe his ears. Jesus of Nazareth, who had once been beloved by the people for his supposed healings and public moral teachings, had now been thrown to the wolves. A man of peace was about to start a war.

"Why? What evil has he done?" Pilate inquired, but the

crowd gave him no answer.

This man's own people had turned against him, and for what? Perhaps this Jesus was not the only madman in Jerusalem. Perhaps it was this entire people who had succumbed to madness.

Pilate summoned one of the attending centurions to his side.

"Beat this man and bring him back to me," Pilate ordered. "But be careful not to kill him. He has not yet been sentenced."

As the Nazarene was taken away, Pilate looked over the crowd. The people were filled with an unquenchable anger, and he could see that the chief priests relished in Jesus' very public humiliation. Their appetites for power had always betrayed them. The image they had carefully cultivated as honorable, holy men had eroded, revealing the truth of their envious hearts. This may not have bothered Pilate if they had not been so previously resolute in their moral outrage. This Christ had exposed the wickedness within them, and it was difficult to restrain such evil upon its release.

Pilate turned from the crowd for a moment only to notice a spectator standing close by. It was his wife's servant, a young girl quietly loitering in the court behind him. Fear of the people had petrified her. Even so, Pilate summoned her to his side to question her privately.

"Why are you here? Is everything alright?"

"I am sorry, my lord," she said, sheepishly. "Your wife, she has an urgent message."

"Can you not see that I am in the middle of a trial? What could possibly be so important to warrant interruption?"

The servant girl cowered a little but spoke anyway. "She knows, my lord. She only asks that I tell you this: 'Have nothing to do with that righteous man, for I have suffered much because of him today in a dream.'"

"Righteous man? You mean Jesus of Nazareth? The one they call Christ?"

She nodded. "Yes, my lord. Your wife has been in anguish all day, having woken from a powerful nightmare. The gods have spoken to her. She says that you should recuse yourself from this man's blood and leave it alone."

"Return to the palace," Pilate ordered. "Tell her to stay out of my affairs."

When Pilate dismissed the girl, he sat back in his seat and thought quietly to himself. The uproar of the crowd faded from his thoughts, and he questioned the nature of the message.

If the gods had indeed sent him this warning, perhaps the best way to convey this to the people was to give them what they desired. Even just a taste of it, and they may soon abandon their request. The prefect ordered the guards to bring to him Barabbas, who was being held not far off. As they fetched him, his centurions returned with Jesus, now quite loosely wearing a purple robe. Blood trailed from each footstep, and the man could hardly stand.

But the most curious detail was the crown of thorns that had been placed on Jesus' head. Pilate stared at Jesus as he slowly ascended the platform. Then, he turned back to the people.

"See, I am bringing him out to you that you may know

that I find no guilt in him," he shouted. "Behold the man!"

The people roared, and as the commotion continued, Barabbas was also brought before them.

"Which of the two do you want me to release for you?" Pilate asked, now standing before the people. On his left-hand side stood Jesus, who spoke not a word to the assembly. His disheveled, bloodied appearance was quite the sight, though none could bear to look on it for too long. To Pilate's right stood Barabbas, who cheered along with the crowd. His warped smile was sickening.

"Barabbas! Barabbas!" they shouted. Even the chief priests and scribes, these supposed holy men of Israel, were calling for the release of a murderer.

"Then what shall I do with the man you call the King of the Jews?"

"Crucify him!" One voice shouted, and soon the rest echoed this sentiment. "Let him be crucified!"

"Why? What evil has he done?" Pilate asked again, but he again received no answer. The crowd only grew louder as the people continued to demand crucifixion. Finally, he relented. "Take him yourselves and crucify him, for I find no guilt in him!"

"We have a law," the long-bearded priest spoke furiously, "and according to that law he ought to die because he has made himself the Son of God!"

First, he is the King of the Jews, and now the Son of God?

There was far more to this Jesus of Nazareth than Pilate understood, and at this point far more than he cared to. The Roman prefect had retreated into his home and brought Jesus along with him. It was one thing for the people to believe that this man was the Christ, their long-awaited king. This could be proven by genealogies and family histories. Jesus may indeed have royal blood dating back to the times of the Hebrew kings. That could certainly prove a problem in itself. But it was another thing entirely to claim the title of "Son of God."

Pilate knew that, for the Jews, a blasphemy like this—if indeed it was a blasphemy—could not be abided. He had been educated in only the basics of Jewish law and could recall enough to know that many had been stoned for far less than equating themselves with the divine. To call oneself a prophet was one thing, but this? This was not something that the people, certainly not the Sanhedrin, would easily let go.

Of course, if Caesar got wind of this, that would ignite a far superior fire. If it became public knowledge that there was another in this region claiming to be the true Son of God, it would look quite poorly on him as well. His failure to keep the peace, to put that sort of idealistic rebellion to death, would surely mean the end of his time as prefect of Judea. It may have even greater repercussions than that.

Beating this man did not seem to change the people's minds. If anything, it only reinforced their demands for his death. But Jesus of Nazareth was no thief. He was no murderer. None of these charges, these attempts to portray him as some bloodthirsty criminal or sickened animal, could stick when speaking with him face to face. Still, something must be done. Something.

Pilate took a deep, long look at Jesus. He stared gravely at the man, looking for any sign of resistance, any hint that he was secretly a zealot or an insurrectionist waiting for his time to strike. There was none. He just stood there, suffering his wounds far better than many of his own men may have in a similar predicament.

"Where are you from?" Pilate finally asked.

He knew that he was from Nazareth, but the man had previously mentioned another kingdom, one far beyond this world. He was curious to see if this Jesus would stick with his story or change it now in the face of crucifixion. But the man did not answer.

"You will not speak to me?" Pilate was beginning to grow impatient with Jesus' lack of common courtesy. "Do you not know that I have the authority to release you or to crucify you?"

Jesus looked up at Pilate, his face painted scarlet with blood. "You would have no authority over me at all unless it had been given you from above."

These were strange words, and yet profound. They cut

deep, as if wedging themselves within Pilate's breast and straight to the heart. It was true that he had been appointed to this post by a higher authority, but that was not the "above" that this Christ seemed to be referring. It became clear to Pilate that this man was not afraid to die, but did that mean he was worthy of death?

Could this be another warning from the gods? Pilate wondered. *Is this a plea from the heavens? Who is this man?*

Jesus continued. "Therefore, he who delivered me over to you has the greater sin."

When Pilate and Jesus returned to Gabbatha, the chief priests swarmed the platform.

"If you release this man, you are not a friend of Caesar's," the long-bearded priest called out to Pilate. Turning to the crowd, he shouted, "Everyone who makes himself a king opposes Caesar!" The rest of the people agreed, crying out once more for Barabbas.

Pilate had had enough. He turned to Jesus and pointed

to him in front of the whole assembly. "Behold your King!" he shouted.

The people continued to rage, the name "Barabbas" foaming from their mouths. They had grown restless and far too tired for any further delays. After all this time, it was surprising that the Jews had not resorted to violence before now, but Pilate could see that was about to change. As Hebrew shoved Hebrew, the people quickly set their sights on the prefect and his soldiers. It was the aqueduct debacle all over again. A riot during Passover could only end in a greater uprising of Jews, something that simply could not be allowed to happen.

Not under his command.

Pilate lifted his hand to calm the crowd. The people continued to mutter among themselves, but they were no longer screaming. They watched carefully as Pilate walked over to the receptacle placed beside his judgment seat and dipped his hands. The cold water was immaculate. The cool touch refreshed his warm, dry hands. He savored the feeling, and the outrage nearly slipped from his mind. This small peace lasted but a moment as he turned to address the people.

"I am innocent of this man's blood. See to it yourselves."

The people roared. "His blood be on us and on our children!" one shouted. The rest echoed the same sentiments. It appeared to Pilate that the people were no longer thinking for themselves; they had let the chief priests and the scribes think for them.

"Shall I crucify your King?" Pilate asked one final time. While he did not want to free Barabbas, he had no true desire to kill the Nazarene either. It had been his hope that the people would relent so he might set the preacher free. He now saw that this was impossible.

"We have no king but Caesar!" one of the chief priests replied, and the rest of them parroted the statement. Men who had previously criticized Caesar for his high taxes, his political overreach, and his audacity to claim himself as "the son of the gods." These same men were now committing themselves in word and deed to the man they had long hated—all because there was another they detested more.

Before Pilate could respond, the people chanted once more for Barabbas. The murderer laughed as the people declared him their new hero, yet Pilate could not help but fix his eyes firmly on the one whose praises they had hailed only days prior. The man was beaten, bloodied, and bore the weight of their guilt on his shoulders.

But there was nothing more that Pilate could do.

The prefect called the captain of his guard to his side. "Give these people what they want," he whispered. "Release the murderer to them."

"And what of this Jesus, my lord?"

"As they say. Prepare him to be crucified." He turned to the man once more, standing there as his own people screamed at him. There was no love in their eyes, no mercy in their hearts. They wished only to see Jesus nailed to the beams reserved only for those Pilate wanted to make an example of. Thieves and murderers. This Jesus was neither, though now he would be murdered as if he were among the worst of them.

Barabbas was unshackled and released into the crowd. As one man regained his freedom, another was taken to the depths of the palace to be beaten and scourged. The Sanhedrin had gotten what they desired after all. They had wanted this man to be punished for his blasphemies, to be sentenced to death for the teachings that threatened their own. Now, he would be. Pilate felt sick. He had washed his hands of this madness, but his mind had become an unquiet tempest. What more could he have done? There was no way to convince the people. Even Caesar himself would have bowed to their demands, if not simply to keep the city from complete destruction.

Never had he felt sympathy for a Jew before now, but the thought of this Christ, this "King of the Jews," would not leave him. It was as if the man haunted him and would continue to do so until his death. Perhaps even after.

He returned to the palace and shut himself indoors. Far away from the agony of the man he had just sentenced to die. The *innocent* man he had allowed the people to kill. *There is no honor in this*, Pilate thought to himself. Though he had physically cleansed himself of the matter before the people, inwardly he burned. He considered returning to the lararium. At the very least, he might look upon the face of the gods and cry out for relief. It may have given him some comfort, if not for just a moment. But he could not bring himself to do so.

No good would come of it.

Instead, Pontius Pilate wandered aimlessly through the palace. He avoided every servant and every guard who sought to bring a matter to his attention. He avoided the hall where he knew his wife was recovering from her dreams, her nightmares. They were now his cruel reality. Had he listened to her, had he simply turned the man loose, he may not be wrestling with this uncharacteristic doubt. His stiff-neckedness had pushed him into further pits of despair, all over a man he did not even know.

Had I not had him crucified, the people would have revolted, Pilate encouraged himself. *The streets would have certainly flowed with blood and flame otherwise.*

More than that, it kept him from any potential review

from Caesar. He could not withstand another mark on his record, not after previous disputes with the people. If they truly wanted this Jesus dead, then this would be the only way to ensure the blame did not fall on him.

Pilate wiped his brow with a wet cloth and held it there to ease his troubled mind. A drink followed, and then another.

"My lord?" Pilate set down his cup and turned to the centurion standing by, one of his faithful guards, Longinus. He was a tall man, and one of the region's best. "The Nazarene has received his lashes, forty minus one. The men have taken him to Golgotha."

The place of the skull, as the people knew it, was a hillside just outside of the city. Many men had died excruciating deaths there, and many more would undoubtedly follow. Pilate rose and left his cup behind, following Longinus down the palace, through the courtyard, and to this horrid hill. A trail of blood led them there, as it had seeped into both sand and stone.

The Nazarene had been properly beaten. The thorny

crown had sunk into his flesh and was now twisted in his hair. Individual thorns had broken off the makeshift crown and embedded themselves within his forehead and skull. His eyes could hardly stay open.

The Sanhedrin were standing not far off, taking precautions not to bloody their own hands any further. As far as Pilate was concerned, there was not enough water in the world to cleanse them of the bloodguilt. He turned to Longinus and spoke with a voice loud enough to be heard by the chief priests nearby.

"Bring me a tablet," he ordered. The centurion complied and soon returned with a wooden carving pulled from one of the nearby beams. He handed it to the prefect, who required a tool to write with. Upon receiving one, he wrote an inscription on the wood, first in a language the Jews would recognize, but then in Latin and Greek also.

It was a simple phrase, one that none of the Sanhedrin would easily forget. For those who believed that this Jesus was their long-prophesied king, this would dispel those beliefs and crush any further rebellion. Yet, there was another purpose for Pilate's words.

Pilate had secretly been amazed by this Nazarene. Jesus never once begged for his life, and in the brief moments they had spoken, the prefect saw something in this Christ that he had seen in few others besides himself. He was a man of authority. Whether it was misplaced or not was of no consequence. Jesus believed the words he spoke. They were his and his alone, and this could not be taken from him—not even in death.

Pilate did not believe that Jesus of Nazareth was the rightful ruler of Jerusalem. Though agreeing with the Jews was an unusual occurrence for him, even they had acknowledged that there was no other king but Caesar. But there was something about this man that he could not explain. Perhaps he was of royal blood, but that blood had been largely drained from his flesh and bone.

Pilate handed Longinus the inscription, reading, "This is Jesus of Nazareth, the King of the Jews." He ordered the centurion to see it nailed into the top of the Nazarene's cross. As expected, the religious elite soon spoke up.

"Do not write, 'the King of the Jews!'" screamed Caiaphas' top man from afar. He had seen the letters on Pilate's inscription and was further enraged. "Rather that, 'This man said, I am King of the Jews.'"

Pilate turned to the Sanhedrin with a tired glare. He was weary of their requests, their complaints. Had the gods ordered it, he would have struck them down this instant for their presumptions. As if they could order him around like some Jewish dog who followed closely at every word.

"What I have written, I have written."

There was no need for Pilate to oversee the crucifixion itself. His men were more than capable of that, and besides, his part in this trial was done. It was time to put this Jesus of Nazareth out of his mind and return his attention to the city at large. It was then that his thoughts fell to the issue of Barabbas.

This murderer had been released into Jerusalem and had likely already reunited with the same brood of zealots who desired to see Rome overthrown. This was a mess. If he was not careful, he would have a riot on his hands anyhow, and the difference would be catastrophic.

Barabbas and his men were not simple Jews who would only push back against those who threatened their basic livelihood. They were fanatics who would fight to the last man for the sake of the "glory of Israel." (Looking around the city, Pilate was unsure what that even meant.) In word, the zealots cared about their religious law the same way the Pharisees and Sadducees did. But in deed, they were far more willing to shed innocent blood than even some of Pilate's own men.

No, he could not allow a man like Barabbas, one whom the people rallied behind so quickly, to walk free. Something must be done about him; the question remained how to proceed.

Nothing could be done until after the Passover. With so many Jews here from across the region, any significant militarized push against the zealots (or those who may be suspected of harboring such radical ideals) would only fuel a greater fire than Pilate had an interest in igniting. This next course would need to be a careful one. He would have to consult some of his local spies. They might have insight on both Barabbas' whereabouts and the schemes of those who affiliated with him.

This, of course, would be tomorrow's problem, for just as Pilate had resigned himself to any thought of the crucified "King of the Jews," he looked out to the west toward Golgotha. As suddenly as a winter storm, the sky grew dark. Clouds unraveled like scrolls across the heavens, and the sun was hidden from his eyes.

Was it an eclipse?

A thick desert storm?

He could not tell.

One thing he did know was that Sol's reach had been cut off by this thickness, and though Pilate was the most powerful man in all Jerusalem, no order he gave could dispel it.

Though unable to bring back the light of day, Pilate was not entirely helpless. He ordered the torches to be lit throughout the palace. It was a strange occurrence, this sudden dark. It reminded him of one of the Jewish legends, particularly the one about their favorite prophet, Moses. From what he recalled, a similar darkness fell over Egypt as a sign of judgment from Israel's single God. No doubt, these people remembered the legend themselves and had scattered like field mice the moment the sun escaped from their view. Pilate was not fearful of this strange phenomenon, though it did deeply unsettle him. It was only the sixth hour of the day, and there was no logical reason that the sky would turn so suddenly to black. It was baffling to the man, but he carried on anyhow.

Though many of his soldiers and servants stood looking westward from where the darkness first crept, he ordered them back to their duties. Pontius Pilate was a harsh taskmaster, and so his orders were carried out with little to no resistance.

That was the sort of power that money could not buy, Pilate thought. *It could only be appointed by the gods themselves.*

As the day pressed on, so did its woes. After some time

working in the dark, Pilate recused himself to dine when the walls and ground around him began to quake. This was far more unsettling than the sudden darkness. Statues crumbled, cups burst, and the prefect himself nearly fell to the ground as it moved beneath him. His anger was kindled, but he was unsure at whom he should direct it. This was not the work of the Sanhedrin, though his inflamed thoughts turned at first to them. It was also not the fault of his servants, whom he chastised for their slowness when it came to tending to him and the dining room.

There was a far greater power at work here.

Soon after the earthquake, Pilate found himself outside in the courtyard. As it was the Day of Preparation, some of the Jews had sent word to Pilate, asking that the legs of those being crucified (for there were two others alongside Jesus) be broken. He honored their request and was soon left alone.

Evening quickly came, though after the previous bout of darkness, Pilate didn't see much of a difference. While the hot desert sun was nowhere to be seen, the dense, sandy air was as uncomfortable as ever. Still, there he sat in the courtyard, surrounded by the shadowed trees, which again stood as the guardians of his mental faculties. If they had been men, he would have had them killed for negligence. He did not feel any more at peace with them standing guard as he had wandering the halls of the praetorium by his lonesome. Even more frustrating was that they did not fend off any unwanted visitors.

When Pontius Pilate looked up from the troubled waters of his mind, he saw two of his men standing before him. One was Longinus, who had returned from Golgotha. With them was another man, clearly a Jew, who stood quietly. It was obvious from his robes that this was a respected man. Like some of the Sanhedrin from before, Pilate recalled his face, but only faintly. He sighed deeply before addressing him.

"Have I not done all that you people have already asked? What more might I do?"

"Forgive me the intrusion, prefect," the man spoke. As he did, he looked over his shoulder, as if he were afraid of being watched. "My name is Joseph, and I have come to discuss an urgent matter."

"Where are you from, Joseph?"

"Arimathea, a small town to…"

"I know where it is. You are a member of the Sanhedrin, is that right?"

Joseph nodded.

"Where are the rest of your people?"

"They do not know I am here. I and a select few are ashamed of what our brethren have done this day. It is with this heaviness that I come with a small request."

"You people and your requests," Pilate muttered to himself. "What is it you would ask?"

"For his body, sir. I have set aside my own tomb for the man, Jesus of Nazareth, and I wish to acquire his body from your guard so that we might give him a proper burial. As you know, the Sabbath is nearly upon us. I would see to it that he is buried properly before then."

"You come to me for a body while it still hangs?"

"You misunderstand, prefect," Joseph spoke firmly.

"Jesus of Nazareth is dead."

Pilate stood at the news. "Dead? Already?"

It had only been a few hours since Pilate had ordered the man to be crucified. Though he had been severely beaten, this was the case with many men who suffered such a fate. Yet, death hardly came so quickly for those nailed to the wooden beams. It often took several hours, sometimes even days, for men to die. There was nothing honorable about it. Men would choke on their own blood as they struggled to inhale, each time tearing larger holes into their pierced hands and feet. Eventually, they would not have the strength to even attempt another breath. Death would take them slowly as their souls fell into a deep and lasting sleep, their bodies drained of any lingering life.

He turned to Longinus and summoned him closer. "Is what this man says true?"

Longinus spoke up. "It is, my lord." He showed the prefect the bloodied lance in his hand. "We went to break the men's legs as you commanded, but when we saw that the Nazarene was already dead, there was no need for us to do the same to him. Instead, I pierced his side, and both blood and water flowed out."

"Fascinating. He was dead already?"

"Yes, my lord."

Pilate didn't know why, but he was reminded of some of the few words that Jesus had spoken to him earlier. Words about a kingdom… He turned back to Joseph. "You would take his body into your own tomb? Why?"

Joseph stood straight. The man did not seem to be hiding anymore. "You yourself named him the King of the Jews, you must know." He spoke with clarity and firmness that reminded Pilate of the Nazarene. "A king deserves a proper burial."

"King or not, he shall have it," Pilate ordered. He turned to Longinus. "See to it that this man gets the body of the one they call Christ. Do not allow it to anyone else."

"Thank you, prefect," Joseph replied. "May our God bless you."

"I do not require it. Now, go."

Pilate was grateful to be free of the Nazarene once and

for all. Now that the man was dead, and his body taken care of, there was no reason that he should need to hear the name Jesus of Nazareth again. He was hopeful that his wife, whose judgmental gaze he had purposely evaded all afternoon, would let this troublesome figure go.

There may not have been a clear reason to crucify Jesus, despite the contradicting charges of blasphemy and sedition, but what was done was done. Nothing he nor the gods could do would alter that course now, and Pilate knew that dwelling on the possibilities of a different past was a fleeting exercise that could just as easily break a man as the sword. He had made his decision; he had washed his hands of the bloodguilt that some would undoubtedly hold over him. He had put an end to a riot before it began. For such a turbulent time as Passover, he had done quite well.

That evening, Pilate slept. He did not dream; he did not wrestle in his sleep. He simply closed his eyes, let the darkness wash over him, and allowed time to run its natural course. When he did awake, he did so knowing that it was a new day. Sol had proven faithful, and he rose early to take in the warm rays breaking through the palace windows. Strangely, he was invigorated by the simple beauties amid such an anthill of a city, though he still longed for his palace in Caesarea. He would be there soon enough.

It shouldn't have surprised Pilate that his morning routine was once again interrupted by the Jews. They had become quite pestilent and even after a full night's rest, he became irritated by their insatiable demands. Upon being summoned from the breakfast table by one of his guards, Pilate regrettably met select members of the Sanhedrin out in the palace courtyard.

"Is it not your Sabbath?" The prefect mocked. "The man you call the King of the Jews is dead. What more could you desire?"

"We did not call him 'the King of the Jews,'" snarled the long-bearded priest, the same figurehead as before. Pilate would not be bothered to learn his name, certainly not after the events of the past day. "That was a title that you wrote for him."

"Speak plainly. What is it you want now? I am not a

slave that you may summon without consequence, and I grow weary of these games."

"Sir, we remember how the imposter said while he was still alive, 'After three days I will rise.'" The priest could tell that Pilate did not care enough to ask what this meant, and so he continued. "Therefore, order the tomb to be made secure until the third day, lest his disciples go and steal him away and tell the people, 'He has risen from the dead,' and the last fraud will be worse than the first."

Pilate could not help but laugh.

If Augustus Caesar—*may he live forever*—did not march triumphantly out of his own tomb, there was no way that a traveling preacher from Nazareth of all places would do so. He looked around at the soldiers standing by, likewise stifling their amusement, and motioned toward them.

"You have a guard of soldiers," he exclaimed. "Go, make it as secure as you can."

Pilate ordered that an imperial seal be attached to the tomb—and with that, he retired indoors. Whether Jesus' followers stole his body or not was of no concern to him, and he certainly did not care if the priests were unsettled by these sorts of religious claims. Even if Jesus himself were to walk out of his tomb, alive and well, Pilate was finished with hearing about the man from Galilee. This was but a day in the many years of Pilate's rule, and there were far more important matters for him to attend to.

As he walked the halls, returning to the dining room, Pilate passed Longinus, whose eyes were fixed westward as he gazed through a nearby window.

"Longinus?" Pilate barked. "Why are you not at your post?"

"Forgive me, my lord," the centurion bowed. "I was only thinking on the crucifixions."

"What of them? Have you not seen dozens with your own eyes?"

"Yes, my lord, I have."

"Then what more is there to think about?" Pilate turned and began to start down the hall before Longinus spoke up.

"He was not a criminal, my lord. He was a man who was loved by the people."

"Yes," Pilate said, turning back to his officer. "And it was those very people who turned on and crucified him."

"I saw some of his followers at Golgotha, my lord. They were weeping, and yet, in his agony, this man Jesus spoke kindly to them. He offered his mother comfort by binding one of his disciples to her. He could not have cared less about his own body." Pilate listened closely as the centurion continued. "As we mocked him and bargained for his clothes in front of him, he did not curse us as the other two men did. He did not hate us or wish us ill. He prayed and asked his God, this one God whom the Jews serve, to have mercy on us."

"He sounds like a fool."

"He sounded like a god, sir. Perhaps even the Son of God."

"Enough. You will not speak any more of this Jewish rabble. You know as well as I that there is only one son of the gods, and that is Caesar."

Longinus stepped forward, an ounce of fear in his step. He thought twice before uttering these next words.

"Yes, my lord. And yet, at the death of this man, the earth trembled, the sky blackened, and tombs were split open like a broken dam. I cannot comprehend these things. They are far too amazing for man to understand."

"Return to your post, Longinus. You would be best to forget the day."

"Yes, you may be right," the centurion replied. "And yet, I fear that I will never be the same."

TO WASH ONE'S HANDS

Afterward

It is believed that Pontius Pilate served as governor over Judea from 26 to 36 A.D., when he was removed from office after ordering a group of Samaritans killed in Ti-rathana. In his *Antiquities of the Jews*, Josephus records that many surviving Samaritans sent word to the governor of Syria, Lucius Vitellius, accusing Pilate of murder. Vitellius ordered Pilate to return to Rome to plead his case before Caesar Tiberius, and he obeyed. However, by the time that Pilate finally made it to Rome, Tiberius was already dead. This would have been approximately three years after Pilate ordered the crucifixion of Jesus Christ.

Not much is known about Pilate's life after this, though he never returned to Judea.

While there is some debate about whether this was

his decision or the ruling of Tiberius' successor Caligula, the truth is that his decade of service in the Ancient Near East is largely remembered due to his brief encounter with Christ. Because of this, we know little more about what became of him—though there are some theories.

In his *Ecclesiastical History*, the fourth century church historian Eusebius cites "tradition" as his source for his claim that Pilate killed himself after being disgraced after his return to Rome. This event is said to have taken place in 39 A.D., though there is little historical evidence in support of it. Many have since argued that it is more likely that Pilate retired into obscurity, having been humiliated after being called to Rome.

Conversely, others, such as the first- and second-century Christian apologist Tertullian, believed that Pilate saw the error of his ways and converted to Christianity sometime after these events. Tertullian notes that, claiming to have seen Pilate's own report to Caesar Tiberius concerning Christ, "[he had] become already a Christian in his conscience."

Likewise, Church tradition states that this experience convinced Pilate's wife—who goes unnamed in the scriptures but has come to be known as "Claudia Procula" in the Western canon—to adapt the Christian faith as her own. In the Eastern Orthodox and Catholic traditions, as well as in the Ethiopian and Coptic Churches, Procula is considered a canonized saint, while the Western Church does not believe there is sufficient evidence concerning her supposed faith.

To this end, Pilate's private thoughts about Christ remain a mystery. Yet, interestingly, apart from Jesus and the virgin Mary, Pontius Pilate is the only human person named in some of the Church's oldest creeds.

The Nicene Creed states that, "For our sake He was crucified under Pontius Pilate." Similarly, the Apostles Creed asserts that, "[Christ] suffered under Pontius Pilate, was crucified, died, and was buried." Two millennia after Pilate ordered Jesus to be scoured and crucified, the Roman prefect is still famous for being the man who saw to it that Christ was put to death. His story remains both a cautionary tale and a challenging indictment of a man who the historical record largely forgot.

Lastly, you may be wondering about Longinus.

Though he goes unnamed in the four canonical Gospel accounts, various apocryphal sources (namely the non-canon Gospel of Nicodemus, sometimes called the Acts of Pilate) and Church tradition have come to refer to him as Longinus. Under this name, he has been venerated as a saint in the Catholic, Anglican, and Orthodox traditions. While it is unknown if Longinus truly became a Christian (the Bible is not clear, despite his apparent confession that Jesus is "the Son of God" at the foot of the cross), for the purposes of this tale, it was important to emphasize the two paths that Pilate—and frankly, all of us—may take in regard to Jesus.

We can either be like those who turned on Christ, betraying Him to the point of death while refusing to acknowledge His role as the Son of God, or we can confess Him as the true Lord over all, forsaking our own sin in obedience to the Savior.

As the Apostle Paul wrote in Romans 10:9, "…If you confess with your mouth that Jesus is Lord and believe in your heart that God raised Him from the dead, you will be saved."

ABOUT THE AUTHOR

Michael John Petty is an award-winning author, screenwriter, podcaster, and filmmaker with a B.A. in Film & Photography from Montana State University. When he isn't writing, he enjoys scenic drives, mountainous hikes, fellowship with his local church, and a good Western. Michael is the creator of The Bear-tooth Mountain Archive, which began with *The Beast of Bear-tooth Mountain*. His short story, *The Devil's Left Hand*, was awarded the Spur Award for Best Short Fiction in 2025. You can subscribe to his newsletter, *Further Up & Further In*, on Substack.

He currently resides in North Idaho with his wonderful wife and beautiful daughters.